"Hate is a Disease that Love Can Cure"

Theophilus Momo-Yande Kamara

content

Page 1.. The Sick king & His 3 Servants
page 4.. The Preacher and the Ganjer Dealer
page 6.. "Never Sell Yourself to Win the Heart of a Nation"
page 8.. The Royal Seeds Of Aberdeen Chiefdom
Page 9.. The Apple Tree Farmer and His Two Sons
Page 10.. Unsatisfied Lover
Page 13.. The Inquisitive Bird that Couldn't Handle
   the Wave of the Wild Winds
Page 15.. The Midget that Try to Look Over a Giant Shoulder
page 16.. "The Royalty From Banana Island"
Page 18.. "The Brave Hunt "
Page 20.. "The Stubborn Lion"
page 22.. "Kehleh & Meleh"
Page 27.. Mamboya"
Page 61.. "Hate is a Disease that Love can Cure"
Page 65.. The Reason Why the Birds and Ants are Always
   After the Termites and The Worms
Page 67.. Let if Fly if It has Wings
Page 69.. Burden From our Past

My Life Angel

Like a gleams of light from the heaven,
the attribute of your pregnancy spark the glow of your purity.
And like the sunrise above, the beauty of life grow within your rich womb.
My presence in your belly create an unrest state of mind
and those physical and emotional pain create tide waves like the ocean
Each day you fought through the struggle to nurture me with constructive principles
My courage, my shield, the gate of joy.
You're my underground tunnel with a promising light.
You birth me through pain to see the light of heaven on Earth,
and on sleepless night and exhaustion, you manage to carter to me.
You stress and cry when I'm sick,
You discipline me even when it hurt you to do so
and I appreciate it Mama, because it take a pressure to crack a nut.
You've dug me through life trenches with your patent, faith, courage and action,
and let me know that even if the world is against me,
you'll stand beside me as my refuge.
We sometime differ through opinion, but we're always friend through mother and child bond.
We elevate through each other.
My failure is your misery, and your sadness is my weakness.
My light, my joy, my friend, my queen, my pain.
You're my foundation and the nourishment of life,
without you, life won't exist
The golden womb of humanity.
I love you MAMA.

The Sick King & His 3 Servants

Once upon a time in a kingdom similar to ours, lived a mighty king named Shaku who ruled bravely for many years. He was highly respected by his people for his brave leadership contribution.

Despite his brave and loyal service toward his people, he was a sick king who couldn't bear a child who would replace him as king.

As the king grow old, and his conditions grew worse. The people of the town grew worried about the future of the kingdom.
He knew his destiny and knew the throne is for the taking. He was aware of the fact that the kingdom would fall into the hands of an unprepared leader and destroy all the greatness the empire had previously gained. So he decided to hand over the throne to one of his loyal servants.
The potential candidate choosing for the position were his maid, his chief and his messenger.

The night before the ceremony, the king hosted a feast for the servant, where he provided a delicious meal, but not a single drink was given to digest the meal.
After the feast, each servant was provided with a luxurious room inside the palace, and in each room lay a battle of seal wine. The maid saw it as an opportunity to fill his thirsty craving, so he grabbed the wine, unsealed it and drank every drop of it. The chief also saw it as an opportunity to fill his thirst and to increase his knowledge over the competition, so he unsealed the wine and drank as he please.

The messenger saw the wine and acknowledged the fact that he was still a servant under a king's palace. He realize the day haven't arrive for him to ignore his servant role and make decisions on his own without the king's permission.

The morning soon arrived and people from all over the town soon crowded in front of the king's palace to witness and celebrate the new king. Looking at the impatient crowd , the sick king then call one of palace guards and ordered him to call all 3 servants, and for all 3 men to bring along with them their wine.

All 3 men arrive as the king ordered, but only the messenger was able to live up to the king demand, so the king then decided to act with precision as any wise king would by questioning the other 2 servant of why they drank the wine?

The maid who was first to reply to the king inquire, stood tall and say, Your highness, since you provided us with a meal without a drink, I assume the wine in the room was meant for us to digest the meal you provided us earlier with.

The king then nodded his head as he turned and faced the other servant, repeating the same question to the chef.
The chef then replied, Your highness, I drank the wine because I thought it would increase my knowledge as a new king..The king then nodded his head for the second time, and turn to face the roaring crowd to address them.
Hearing the maid respond, the king then said, " Okay! So which one two of you didn't drink the wine ?"
The maid, raise his hand and said, "I did not. you highness. For I'm still in your palace as a servant, and still under your leadership as my king, so it is forbidden for a servant to act as he pleases without permission from his master."

The king then smiled, shook his hand and stood at the podium to address the impatient crowd..”My people, in what civilized kingdom does a servant randomly act without the king's permission?”

The crowd then yelled, "No kingdom!"

The king then lowered his voice, saying, "It is true that a dictator is a self pleaser who may employ any means to stay ahead of all, but it is clear to all righteous men and women of this town that it is forbidden in any righteous kingdom that a servant should act on his own in a king palace to please himself without the acknowledgment or permission of the king. Impatient servants who are not aware of things around them and are triggered by narrow vision are poor leaders of a kingdom."

So the king then crowned the messenger saying, "For you have humbly shown great patience, and with patient and effort come knowledge and understanding that exalt a great kingdom. You showed bravery as my servant and were keenly aware of your standing as a servant under my palace. You proved you honor as a loyal servant, because even when face with temptation, you wouldn't exercise your freewill to act in a role not appropriate for you. Therefore, your bravery have exalted you as the new king."

The Preacher and the Ganja Dealer

Once upon a time, there lived a preacher, whose words were as shiny as pearls, but his steps in righteousness were uncertain.

One beautiful Sunday afternoon after a church service, he decided to take a stroll into the slums of the city, known as the ghetto.

While he was there he encountered an old accomplice, a pot dealer named Jankoleko, from whom he purchased a dime sack of marijuana.

As the preacher was purchasing the herb, he said, "My brother, I would like you to come to my church. We definitely have room for sheep like you."

The dealer replied, "Thanks a lot for the invite. I will come when the time is right. But for right now, I have to work to lay a strong foundation for my loved ones."

The preacher smiled and said, "My child, this is not you. I know you're smarter than what you're doing. Look at you! Living in misery, sinning and selling yourself. Don't you feel ashamed of yourself?"

"Ashamed of what? Reality in life? Nah! I'm never ashamed of reality! I accept things as they are and strive to make the best of it. So as you may see, Mr. Preacher Man, I know my actions were not always pure and I don't suggest that anyone else follow my ways. But who is more of a sinner? The poor man struggling to feed; clothe and shelter his kids... or the tongue twisting thief who but pretends to be righteous but is a hypocrite, stealing from the poor and buying substances from survivors like me?"

The preacher smiled, then burst into laughter before he said, "I see where you're going with this, young man." He laughed and smiled again, then said.

"Look, child, this is not about me, I'm just trying to save a lost sheep like you from entering hell."

"Hell, you say?" the dealer asked, looking surprised. "Mr. Preacher Man, you don't know my life... yet you sit here and criticize or try to judge me when you can't even practice what you preach. Your job is simple, pretending and lying to these poor folks to enrich yourself with their money. Mine is dodging bullets, risking my freedom, and avoid getting bitten by leeches. So as you may see, Mr. Man, I'm already living in hell. I'm just trying to find my way to heaven by reaching my dreams, so I can feed, clothe and shelter my loved ones."

There are those who criticize others while forgetting where they themselves stand. If we try to criticize others then we should also be aware of our own faults. As a leader, you have to go to ground to avoid pursuit; you have to reach expectations before others can believe in you as a leader. Leadership is a journey where you invest in building a tower of hope which others can explore for growth.

"Never Sell Yourself to Win the Heart of a Nation"

There once was a land of great wealth called Afrika, which couldn't provide promises to its citizens. With the mineral resources flourishing under its ground, a lack of education posed a great threat to promising future for its citizens.

This land of opportunity became a land of broken dreams. The door that led to other opportunities was void and impossible to reach because the wealth of the land was still untouched.

With no possibility for liberation, many villagers grew worried and angry because education to exalt the village wasn't forth coming . So the golden future that they had intended for their next generation seemed doomed. The villagers began to realize that the only path to elevation was proper education in order to mine the minerals from their land. The people were desperate to strengthen their village.

As the pressure continued to mount, the elders decided to take matters into their own hands by holding a meeting, where all members soon came up with reconstruction plans. They decided it would be brave "not to use old wood to build a firm bridge." In other words it would be in the best interest of the village not to send an adult to a foreign land to study the secret knowledge to rescue their village. The reason was, that person wouldn't live long enough to strength the future generation. So they came to the conclusion that the smartest path was to select a home, where two youth members would be selected for the mission.

And like a sunrise that promises to the early morning, came a promise from the bottom of the pit. A poor widow name Adama, who had three healthy children: Hassan, the oldest, Mohamed, the middle child, and Marie the youngest daughter. Adama ended up being the woman selected for the course.

Excited to be on the path to success, she celebrated that her children would be part of history for a great cause. This was an opportunity of a lifetime. "Free education is always worthy for growth!" she said. But reality soon hit when it was time to choose just two out of her three children for the scholarship. Difficult as the decision was, she closed her eyes and proceeded by accepting the two lucky tickets for two kids which was an opportunity of a lifetime. Because rescue seemed to be at hand for the villagers her kids had a chance to educate themselves and help mine the minerals in their village and thus modernize their community.

She didn't want to feel like a selfish mother, so she talked to Hassan and told him to keep his eyes on the village while his younger brother and sister went to further their education in order to rescue their home. And like any brave eldest son, he accepted the decision his mother had made. Mohamed and Maria soon went on to study, while Hassan stayed home assisting his mother, keeping his eye on the village resources and attending to other village demands.

Maria went to a village in the east to study nursing and business. But like a broken arrow, she failed to hit her target and allowed her environment to get the best of her.

Due to her drug and alcohol abuse and party lifestyle she ended up getting pregnant and having kids. Ashamed of her failure, she tried to hide her Afrikan image by adopting a new image for her kids not to recognize her roots. So she never returned to her village.

As for Mohamed, he went to the village in the west to study law, and returned home. His return brought hope to everyone in the village. The people were so pleased that they ended up appointing him as chief, since he had a foreign education that they greatly viewed as dominant. But that was made up because deep down he was still an old face with new ambition, driven by power and wealth.

With a new agenda, Mohamed stood hypocritical and used his education to brainwash the villagers with lies that led to empty hope, as he stole their wealth and left the village destitute, and doomed to extinction.

The Royal Seeds Of Aberdeen Chiefdom

Once upon a time in the small royal chiefdom of Aberdeen, lived a brave chief named Enoch. He lived with his three beautiful royal children.

Two of his seeds were twin boys named Yaka and Arumah, and the youngest, a princess named Sahehra . Now, it has been proven many times that blood ties strengthen the bond in a family. But in this family, the obsession for power was clearly ripping the brotherly bond apart. Both were anxious to be chosen as the seed for the throne, and jealousy ignited between the two princes.

One afternoon, a bitter argument erupted amongst the two brothers over the right person to be the chief. The argument turned into a fist fight and a wrestling match. They fought until their father, Chief Enoch walked outside his palace to catch some fresh air and stumbled across his two princes fighting in an aggressive manner.

He interrupted their dispute and asked them, "What has triggered such an ignorant act?"

They replied by saying, "The throne is not only a dominant position, but a symbol and reflection of his heart."

Hearing that only caused him to reconsider his decision. Because he came to realize that if they can foolishly wage war between themselves for something that pertained to their own interest, then they wouldn't be able to be fair leaders. And since they were fighting for the same position, both princes should forfeit the royal throne, so peace could be restored between them.

So the chief decided to skip both princes for their power conscious act toward each other and crown Princess Sahehra as the seed to be on the royal throne after his death, since she was the only royal seed who didn't bring disgrace to the royal family.

The Apple Tree Farmer and His Two Sons

Once upon a time there was an apple farmer named Nassimi, who lived with his two sons, Sam, the oldest and Ansu, the youngest. As the years went by, the apple market crashed and the farmer's business was on the verge of foreclosure.

Unable to keep himself afloat in the business world, Nassimi went to his business partner and borrowed money that he couldn't pay back.

Though the weight of his debt was heavy on his shoulders he was still aware of his business obligations, and his responsibility as a father. He didn't want a landslide to crash onto his sons and he feared that now his labor wouldn't be an inheritance for his sons because of his debt.

As a father, he knew his responsibility, which was laying a healthy foundation for his seeds. He didn't want to leave this world with guilt, so he planted two apple seeds for his two sons, and told them to nurture the seeds with water.

Both agreed to do so, but Sam soon ignored his father's words. Only the youngest son Ansu followed his father's advice and watered his seed until it sprouted from the soil.

Nassimi soon died from sickness and the Government seized his fortune and used it to repay his debt to his business partner. After his debt repayment, there was nothing left in his name, but his two sons and the seeds he'd planted for them to hopefully be successful in their personal lives.

The hard work soon paid off from Ansu's efforts because the plant grew into a tree and bore hundreds and thousands of apples that made him successful, while disobedient Sam was left in poverty and distress.

Unsatisfied Lover

Once upon a time lived a beautiful woman named " Marie Meleh" who was married to a hardworking farmer named Sam Palampo. Sam Palampo was a poor farmer. So he wasn't able to offer Marie Meleh gifts of diamonds, but he treated her like the only life on earth. He planted rice and built a small farmhouse for them to live in.

The queen soon died, and the town crier announced that the king would be holding a dancing contest to select his next queen.

Marie Meleh's friend, Tuleffut visited her right away and informed her of the queen's death. Not satisfied with her status, Marie Meleh started to view the queen's death as a perfect opportunity to capture her dreams.

Unhappy to be living at a low status with her farmer husband, Marie Meleh denounced him and decided to enter the contest. As she was planning to enter the contest, her husband begged her not to leave him. He assured her that they would have brighter days. She pushed her husband aside and said, "Get away from me, I'm tired of smelling like mud and fish, I need a real man who is going to cover me head to toes with jewels, something a broke, weak man like you can't afford."

She entered the contest and succeeded in winning the king's heart. She remarried the king and became the new queen. But as time and reality was revealed in front of her eyes, she found that the king was a womanizer who couldn't resist beautiful women. So he abused their marriage with disloyalty, and treated her less than the queen that she had fantasized about.

The king soon told her that he was thinking about having another queen.

Unhappy with the king's intention, she denounced her throne by divorcing the king and returning to her old husband to see if he would forgive her and accept her again. Because the jewels she was seeking brought no joy, but only glitter.

As she arrived, she saw a woman cooking. She paused, before saying, "Excuse me, does Palampo still live here?"

"Oh, you mean Sam Palampo, my husband? Oh yes, he does. He and my son went fishing," the new Mrs. Palampo calmly replied.

As she was finishing her speech, Palampo and his son Suckeya arrived home. "What are you doing here?" Sam Palampo asked.

Marie Meleh turned around and tried to grab his hands, but Palampo pushed her off. She then said, "I just came to say that I'm sorry for my poor decision. You know we're not perfect," she explained.

"I know, that's why I've forgiven you," he replied.

"So does this mean that you will get rid of this mess and accept me back?" she desperately asked.

"Oh absolutely not, I won't live to make the same mistakes. Remember when you told me that you don't need a dirty, fish smelling man like me? Well, guess what?"

"I already know what you're about to say, but all I have to say to you is I am sorry," Marie Meleh said with a sad look on her face.

He looked at her and said, "Apologizing now will let me know that you learned something and you're ready for growth, but it won't change the fact that I'll never love you back the way I once did. It's impossible to recreate those same emotions. Because you created darkness with your unsatisfying ways and insulted me with degrading words and unfaithful ways. This is the woman that brings the light when you create a dark storm. This is the woman who loves me for the person I am, so she is the woman worthy to share the rest of my life with."

"But we did all this hard work to build a dwelling that you're now living in with another woman," Marie Meleh said.

"Well, you gave up, instead of being a little more patient and waiting for harvest. So don't be mad if another woman came and harvested the crops you gave up on," he said as he hugged his new wife Beyah and son Suckeya.

When Marie Meleh heard those words, she knew that there was no chance of winning his heart, so she ran off, disappointed and with tears in her eyes.

Always appreciate what you have, regardless of your expectation of how life should be. Certain things are unworthy until they are lost. So cherish the little things in your possession, whether it glitters or not.

"The Inquisitive Bird that Couldn't Handle the Wave of the Wild Winds"

Once upon a time, a pregnant bird lived high above a palm tree deep in the wild forest. The winter season wasn't too far off, so she bravely stored enough food to sustain her family throughout all of those cold months. She laid three eggs and was very protective of them from other forest creatures. The eggs soon hatched, and two out of the three birds were able to survive.

Winter arrived and the mother's bravery paid off because the family was okay. There was enough food for her and the new chicks. She catered to them like any mother would, but she no longer could stay in the nest, because the food which she had stored for the winter season was now gone, so she had to strive for new food or else they'd starve to death.

So the next day she decided to leave her two boys in the nest to find some food. Before she left, she warned them by saying, "I will be right back, I have to go find food for us to eat. I don't want you two to leave this nest."

"Okay, Ma, we won't," both agreed. So she left to find food.

Hours after her leaving, curiosity started to tempt the two inexperienced chicks. The smaller bird, which was more obedient, listened to his mother's advice and didn't leave the nest. His belief was to first learn from experience and inquire about the wisest steps before exploring the world, or else you will crash.

The elder chick believed that it was necessary to take a risk to see what the world had to offer. So, curious to know what awaited him, he soon realized he could flap his wings. He didn't wait for his mother's permission to leave the nest, he immediately jumped over the side and flapped his tiny wings against the rough wind. Only a few seconds in the wild winds, and the immature bird landed on the ground and became prey for a starving snake.

Their mother returned home and noticed one of her chicks was missing, so she curiously asked the younger chick, "Where is your older brother?"

The younger brother then replied, "He flapped his tiny immature wings against the winds and stumbled to the forest ground, and became a meal for a starving snake."

"The Midget that Try to Look Over a Giant Shoulder"

Once upon a time lived a man named Brahojo, who lived only by his own understanding of the world. As he lived, he ignored the advice of the elders and perceived his own knowledge by acting as he pleased.

One day, Brahojo decided to go to the Makazu forest. As he was gearing up for the journey, the elders from the village came knocking at his door. He opened it and said, "How may I help you?"

"Young one, we came to warn you about the journey you are about to take."

"And what may that be?"

"Well, my son, it seems that the Makazu forest is a forbidden forest, and it has been cursed by our ancestors and it has also been proved numerous times that one individual cannot make it through this forest alone. You need a companion to journey with you and assist you through the trenches dug by our ancestors."

"Hahaha! A companion? Oh no, that's a lie! Men always put their own twist into bringing fear to one's greatness. I came into this world by myself, so I shall take my life journey by myself."

"My child, be careful, even our grand creator that created us had a reason to put companionship on earth. If we didn't need companionship in society, then we'd have been placed on our own planet. So in some way or another, we all need help in life."

"Yeah! But like I said, I came in this world by myself, so I shall strive to conduct my own journey in life," Brahojo yelled as he locked his door and journeyed to this mysterious forest. He fell into a deep ditch, which a single individual couldn't climb out from without the help of a companion above. And with no foreign intervention nor help, he died alone through his own understanding.

"The Royalty From Banana Island"

Once upon a time on the small island of Banana lived a powerful Sierra Leonean chief called "Momo Yande." He ruled for a century without disturbance or any manipulation from his people or any foreigners. Adored by his people for his excellent and effortless work toward society's elevation he bravely dominated his chiefdom and was highly respected for all his great accomplishments.

As he ruled this powerful island, the islanders decided that it was time for the royal treatment. So every home with a virgin teen invited Chief Momo Yande to find his queen. He searched through his invitation homes for his new queen with whom he would extend his royalty. A shy, beautiful young lady by the name of Sameria ended up capturing his eyes. Sameria brought Chief Yande fulfillment and bore him two royal twin seeds, a princess named Oya, and a prince name Tolo.

As Chief MomoYande aged, he decided to send both Oya and Tolo to Moyamba district to study cultural traditions. The two pursued their tasks as ordered by their father, and arrived in a village. As they arrived the villagers sang, danced and offered them great hospitality by preparing their best meals and offering loyalty.

Oya humbled herself and adopted the village hospitality, but Tolo, who was used to the royal and lavish lifestyle wasn't able to adopt to their traditions. So he pushed the villagers off of him, saying, "Do not touch and infect me with disease." His refusal of cultural acceptance created a quicksand hole for himself.

He refused to drink the same water from the well where all the villagers drank from, because he was royalty, so he would only drink the water from the stream that all the kings and royalty drank from.

The princess, on the other hand, humbly restructured firm ground for progress. Like always, she accepted their hospitality, by eating their meals and drinking from both the stream and well water.

As for Tolo, his ego created an illusionary bridge where his refusal created a dead end zone, because soon after the rainy season their stream came to an abrupt end. The stream water ran dry and created a drought for the royalty. So all there was as a source of water was the well water that all the villagers used.

"The Brave Hunt"

Once upon a time there was a tiny bird that lived in the South American jungle. The winter season came and there was a drought. So this tiny bird decided to visit an old hunter friend from the Far East, with whom he could possibly hunt.

Some hours into his journey, the bird soon arrived at his friend's destination where he encountered the same food shortage problem.

With both aware of the drought, they couldn't sit back and starve to death, so they decided to go hunting for food.

While on their hunting quest, they encountered a turtle sitting by the shore of a frozen lake. Stunned by curiosity, the tiny bird then decided to enquire. "No offense, Mister Turtle, but what are you doing standing here in this cold winter weather?" the bird asked.

"Hunting, my friends, feel free to join me on my hunting. There is enough meal beneath this lake for all of us."

"Ha Ha! Hunting you say?" the friend asked, with a funny look on his face.

"Laugh all you want, pal, but there are a lot of fish under this frozen lake."

"Yeah, yeah! I've also heard a similar story about a lazy dog who refused to hunt, so he sat back, patiently waiting for a free meal to come his way, until hunger got the best of him and sent him to his destiny. Death! So save your breath for this chilly weather! I'd rather go hunt in a place where I can see a meal, rather than stick to one place where I can't see a meal and starve to death," the friend replied.

"Well, good luck on your mysterious hunt! Keep in mind that you can't fetch water with a basket. So I'll be right here to hunt where I've seen the sunrise and sunset," the turtle answered.

Hearing them reasoning about their personal decision, the tiny bird then decided that it would be in her best interest to be patient and follow a wise, patient hunter, rather than follow a cocky ignorant hunter driven by impatience.

The bird's decision to stay by the frozen lake only caused the friend to make further inquiry.

"My good ol' friend, I thought you came here to hunt with me?" the friend asked.

"Yes, I came toward your way to hunt for a meal, but if you're not executing wise decisions as a hunter, then it is best that I move toward a promising direction where I can survive."

Hearing the bird respond only gave the friend a reason to further his hunt by himself. Days into their separation, the solo hunter became exhausted from hunting and thirst and didn't have enough zeal to further his hunting quest.

So he dropped down to his knees to catch his last breath. While the two patient hunters who were also in desperation, but brave, preserved their energy at a promising site.

Their patience soon paid off, because the lake where the two hunters had been standing for days on the frozen ice soon melted down and returned to its regular form. Now the two brave hunters hunted and filled their bellies with fish.

"The Stubborn Lion"

Once upon a time, in the wilderness of the Warawara Mountains, lived a dominant lion couple named Cigar, the male, and Lisa, the female lioness who was a few weeks pregnant.

One beautiful Friday evening, the couple decided to relocate to Malama Mountain for safety reasons.

On that particular day, both Cigar and Lisa encountered an obstacle on their long journey. Tommy, who was known for savagely hunting the lions was out in the jungle searching for lions and putting them into captivity.

Tommy soon tracked them and started to chase Cigar. He quickly caught up with and captured Cigar, by shooting him with a tranquilizer gun. He then put him into captivity like the rest of the lions he had captured.

Fortunately, Lisa managed to escape from Tommy, and a few hours later she gave birth to two male lion cubs that she named Bud and Gin.

Lisa went on to raise the two boys successfully without any foreign threat from the other predators in the jungle. She bravely taught them to hunt and survive. But the most important lesson that she taught them was to listen and learn.

Though neither of them knew the true message behind their mother's lesson at that time they proceeded to learn other things in the jungle. But as they went neither was happy with their father absent. Lisa also knew her sons were unhappy, but she didn't know how to approach them with the truth behind their father's disappearance.

One evening, after Lisa got very sick, she decided to tell the boys about their father's disappearance.

Her telling them the true story only left the boys crushed because they cried for hours, but that crying came to a sudden stop when both Bud and Gin came up with a plan to rescue their father who was still in captivity.

They went and told their mother their good scheme that they had devised for their lost father's rescue.

Lisa was happy with the news because she wanted the boys to know their father. So she gave both Bud and Gin her last advice before the two inexperienced souls set out on a two-hour mission.

The advice was for them to, "never drink from the lake close to Tommy's house"—in other words, the zoo house.

"Okay, Mama, we won't," they replied.

"Okay, my brave warriors," she said as she lay down in her sickbed.

They soon left Lisa on her sickbed for the rescue operation. The journey took quite some time, but they eventually arrived at Tommy's penitentiary for lions, where they quickly noticed their father by his scent. He was in very bad condition with the other lions. The two brothers released all the prisoner lions from captivity.

The three quickly got out of Tommy's door and headed for home. Three minutes on their way home, inquisitiveness played its role. Gin, the curious lion, returned and drank from the lake without knowing that Tommy, the lions' nightmare, had poisoned the lake; and eleven minutes later, Gin took his final breath.

"Kehleh & Meleh"

Once upon a time in the small village of Wataloo, lived two friends named Kehleh and Meleh who shared an interest in fishing. As they grew, so did their ambition.

One evening, the two friends decided to head to the Saweh River to fish. On their way, they came to a small bamboo house by the roadside and they immediately stopped to encounter an older woman sitting under a huge cotton tree and chewing her cola nut and drinking palm wine.

They stopped, greeted her and asked her for water.

"Greeting to you wise one and precious mother of this Earth! My name is Kehleh and this is my friend Meleh."

"Oh, greeting to the light of tomorrow!" she said with a bright smile on her face.

"How can we be when you're the structure of society?" Mehleh asked with a shocked look on his face.

The old woman smiled and said, "My name is Oya Sama . Indeed, adults are the guardians of society's structure, but the youth are our investment for the future."

"Well, it is an honor, wise one. You elders see the sunrise before us youth."

"Oh yes indeed," she said nodding her head.

"Wise one, we're dying of thirst. Do you have any water for us?"

"Hold on my children," she said. She pulled out her jar and poured some water into a wooden cup and gave it to them.

They drank, and as they were drinking she started to enquire like any inquisitive person would. "My children, if I may ask, where are you two young men heading to?" she asked.

"Thank you for the water, Mammy Oya Sama . We're going to the Saweh River to fish," Kehleh said.

"Wow, oh how nice, my children. You guys will definitely catch fish, but be careful."

"Oh we will, right now our ambition is strong. Nothing can stop us. We're too gigged up," Mehleh said with much ego.

"Well, my children, ambition is always good, but too much ambition without limitation is like digging a hole for yourself to stumble on," she calmly advised them.

"Thanks, wise one for the advice and thanks a lot for the water. It has definitely boosted our zeal," they said.

"The pleasure is mine, my sons," she said as she sipped her palm wine and chewed her cola nut.

As they sat down to rest and fill their thirst with water, the old lady bit her cola, stared at them and said, "You two young men seem brave, but I hope you guys are brave and appreciative to finish what you've already started. That's what they all say. Just don't be too blind to appreciate what is in front of you like the old folks who once lived in this village.

"Well, my children, our ancestors used to tell us a tale about a group of villagers with mixed emotional feelings.

"One day, the villagers of this town decided to grow corn, rice and peanuts. As the season flew by the village started to experience drought during the growing season. So the villagers grew worried that their crops wouldn't have enough water to grow and produce.

"As their concerns grew, the great Lord decided to answer their prayers and grant them their wishes. A huge storm came pouring down rain on their village for days. As the storm raged, some villagers showed their appreciation by thanking the Lord for the rain, and others showed no appreciation by complaining that it was too much rain. They can't do anything.

"With the complaint, the great Lord intervened to give them a solution. He first separated the villagers by placing all those who were complaining about the rain on dry land where there was no water. Their crops weren't able to grow, so food became scarce in this new land til hunger and death stripped them.

"While the others who smiled and celebrated the rain were able to grow their crops, feed their livestock and sustain their trades and flourishing lifestyle."

"Interesting tale, Oya Sama," they said. "It's really educational. Thanks a lot for sharing it with us."

"Oh yes, whatever educational structure I can lend in support of youth is my pleasure. For even a flower cannot grow by itself without the support of the sunlight and water."

"Thanks, wise one. We really appreciate the lecture. Sometimes we just have to appreciate what is in front of us and get the best of it. Nothing is perfect. Complaint can be a heavy burden."

As they prepared to leave they said, "Well thanks a lot again, but we've to further our quest now. "

"Safe journey, my children," she said as she continued chewing her cola nut.

They soon left the old lady and continued their fishing quest. An hour later, they took a wide turn to the east that sent them in a direction that led to two separate river paths. One was a river path called "Durtee Waf River." At that point to the east a big barracuda resided, but on this river one should always be aware because the weight of the barracuda could be too heavy for the line, and if you're not aware of the weight on the fishing line, you could be dragged back into the water and become a meal for those huge barracuda.

The river path to the west was called "Beyaa Waf River" and it is where snapper swim along and it is guaranteed to satisfy you for a day or two. Moreover, there is always the promise of a safe return on every trip because the size of the fish are too small to outweigh the line.

The two decided to journey their separate ways. Meleh went to the east saying, "Snapper are too tiny for my belly and it will take a dozen of them to equal one barracuda meal."

His ambition for a big catch, however, only weakened his thin fishing line and he later encountered an obstacle that made its return impossible.

As for Kehleh, he was cautious in his approach, so he headed to the west where the tiny snapper posed no safety threat to any. So he was able to fill his basket with a dozen snappers that he took home.

"We the hunters can be the hunted if we're not fully aware of the weight of our pursuit. And in life you never want to pursue something that can change the outcome of your desire."

Jungle Inspiration

Most situations in life are like the zoo where you're placed into captivity to support the supreme beliefs and benefits of the owners and their associates. Animals in the zoo are fed to be lazy and to be dependent on the zookeepers since they need those animals for their own interests, but they are not given enough food to gain strength to break out of the zoo to their freedom. Keep in mind, "A monkey in the jungle has more freedom than a tame monkey in the zoo who is constantly fed to be lazy and miserable." So my advice for you is not to trap yourself in someone's system, liberate yourself and explore the jungle through your own freewill.

Any system that causes you to anchor yourself down in life like a wrecked ship is not worth chasing nor holding on to, but if it can help you sail to your dreams without a regret in your conscience, then it is well worth pursuing.

"Mamboya"

"Moonlight Glimpse at Cape Sierra Shoreline"

Chapter 1

Once upon a time on a pristine stretch of shoreline of Cape Sierra Beach in Aberdeen, Sierra Leone, lived a mixed cultural tradition of all sorts of creatures including humans, who were the overall dominant rulers of this town. The leprechauns were mysterious night crawlers that moved swiftly during the dark to steal food from the humans. Their sneaky ways and creepy image made them the outcasts of society.

"He's a monster. A thief that steals our food every night. He even stole gold and other items," someone accused.

"Kill him!" a man yelled.

"Yeah, let's crush him," the crowd shouted as they stomped, kicked and punched this young father leprechaun that was trying to steal food for his family.

Tycoma's father, Bamo, was executed by the villagers when caught stealing food for his newest boy, also named Tycoma. Tycoma grew up not having a father figure, but his mother Yaema did the best she could to raise Tycoma. But even her best wasn't enough because an uproar soon erupted amongst the villagers who accused Yaema of being a witch. The accusation forced her into a trial and if found guilty of the crime, she would be stoned to death.

"She is a witch!" an old male yelled.

"I am not a witch, but a magician!" she said in her defense.

"She is a witch. Stone her to death!" the old man yelled.

With no solid proof of their claim but because they believed some practiced magic, they stoned Tycoma's mother to death.

With no one to defend her she was stoned to death in front of her newborn baby Tycoma.

Chapter Two

The moon is always full of life. It is the guide for all creatures. And every full moon, strange creatures from every corner of this land would celebrate their freedom from humans. Humans are considered savages who pick on others including their own to criticize, judge and harm. So all these strange crossbreed creatures with one leg, were half human and half animal. Some with human faces and animal bodies, others with human shapes with horns, some with a long shaped body and one eye and some with long legs and little bodies. Each with its own unique magical power would perform their powers as a form of celebration.

One beautiful moonlit evening, the young princess from the sea world named Mamboya decided to go play with her cousin Dafu.

Mamboya swam along the sea world with her cousin. She stopped and treaded water. Bored, she muttered, "We do the same things all the time. I want to see or do something different. Something interesting."

"So what you're saying is that we don't do interesting activities?" Dafu asked.

"I'm not saying that, it used to be fun, but now it's getting boring," she explained.

"Oh wow, Mamboya!"

"Yes, wow. But look, Dafu, you can come with me and explore life or you can stay in this boring place."

"Nah I can't, Papa won't let me," Dafu said.

"Well, I will be right back. I'm heading to the shoreline to meet a friend," Mamboya said as she swam away to the top.

"Hey!" she yelled with a loud echo in the cave.

Tycoma jumped. "What are you doing here, Fishwoman?" he asked.

"I am a mermaid, not a fish woman," she said.

"Well, you look like a fish and you're a woman. So doh, fish-woman," he said.

"Haa! How silly. I am a mermaid," she argued.

"Okay, Ms. Mermaid. What are you doing here in my lucky cave?" he asked.

"How pleasant. Okay let's be specific here, my name is Mamboya. Now, what are you doing at my resting place with all these items? Oh I get it, you stole it from others," she accused.

"I didn't steal them," he said, defending himself as he jumped and grabbed his bags filled with stolen items.

"Oh yes you did," Mamboya said, pointing her finger at him.

Tycoma raised his hand and said, "Okay, okay. I did, but that's because I was given an order to do so."

"An order?" Mamboya asked.

"Yes, you see our world is different, we're considered monsters by the humans, so for us to survive we have to cross their boundary swiftly and get what we need to survive. Humans are often distracted by glitters so we use our magical power to spread gold and diamonds to distract them and steal their food at night."

"How interesting," she said as she pointed her finger at him. "How about you guys just grow your own crops rather than stealing their food," she further suggested.

Tycoma nodded his head and said, "Then there would be clear evidence that we exist. We don't want them to know that we exist because if they do then they will enslave or exterminate us."

"Okay. Now I see your point," she replied.

Tycoma stood tall and said, "Exactly. These people are wicked to their own kind. What makes you think people like us belong in their world?"

"What a messy world. Who civilized them?" Mamboya asked.

"Themselves, that why it is hard to find a common ground. Everybody wants to be in charge," he replied.

"Quick question, Mamboya."

"I'm all ears, Tycoma."

"You're a mermaid?" Tycoma asked.

"Yes, what about it?" she asked.

"How did you do that?" he said, furthering his curiosity.

"Did what?" she asked.

"Turn your tail to human legs."

"Well, that's a secret for only the mermaid," she said with a smile.

"C'mon, please," he begged.

"Oh, relax, it's as easy as breathing," she said as she whipped her hair.

"But how, if I may ask?" he insisted.

"Well, you dry off first then flop your tail three times and your tail turns into human legs," she answered and she walked around the cave.

THE PROPHECY

Tycoma wandered around the cave, and stared at Mamboya before saying, "So it's true!"

"True about what?" Mamboya asked, not knowing what direction he was heading.

"The prophecy."

"What prophecy?" she asked with a surprised look on her face.

"Whoa. Don't tell me you don't know."

"Know what? Look! You're creeping me out now," Mamboya said with a scary look on her face.

"Noo. You don't need to be afraid. Even a prophecy has its destiny."

"What foolish prophecy are you talking about?"

"The prophecy about this…" he said.

"For thousands of years, the Queen of the Dark from a superstitious world lost her magical power to a higher power over a dispute that resulted in her getting one side of her face burned. So for the past one thousand years, the queen had tried numerous times to regain her power through human sacrifice, but nothing has worked in her favor and according to the Book of Wisdom, only a creature from the sea world with a human shape can restore her power."

"Who is she? And where did she came from?" Mamboya asked.

"Her name is Adama and her origin is unknown. All we know is she lives for every thousand years and goes through transformation by entering a young woman's belly and impregnating her. She devises fury, rage and violence so she exterminates anyone who poses a threat to her. She is known in the dark world as the Witch Queen. Adama KohKoh is what she is known as. She has one sister named Yaema who she is jealous of. She knows of her sister being a witch queen, so she moved to the brighter side after moving to another town and became born again."

With a shocked look on her face, Mamboya jumped before asking,

"What? What are you saying?"

"You fit the description of the sacrifice she needed," Tycoma said as he bit his cola nut.

"No I don't. She needs to look somewhere else," she said with a disgusted look on her face.

"Oh yes. "You're the perfect one," Tycoma said, nodding.

"So what kind of sacrifice?" she curiously asked.

Tycoma cast his eyes down and said, "Well, this may sound disturbing, but she needs to kill you and drink your blood."

"Oh noo! I have to get out of here. This is a savage world indeed."

Chapter Three

Though the prophecy was revealed to her, the distraction from the superstitious world incarcerated her emotions.

Mamboya was amazed by Tycoma's magic, she got drawn into his tricks and couldn't blink nor distance herself from him. They became closer than ever and he revealed his secrets to her. His honesty paid off because she soon fell in love with him for his tricks and his courage to share his knowledge.

"You know fear is something we all can overcome. When I was trapped in the sea world based on fear, I held back and didn't cross other boundaries, so I wasn't able to see this side of the world. It is beautiful you know. It might not please all savages who lived here but it surely is wonderful for me," she explained.

"Well, I'm glad that you like it out here. It can be crazy at times, but you will love it. It's good air."

"Haha, very funny. But true. You know one thing I admire about you is the fact that you're willing to share," Mamboya said.

Tycoma smiled and said, "Well, if we all learn to share, all our questions will be answered."

Mamboya nodded her head and said, "Oh yes, but sometimes we have to be careful of whom we choose to share with. Because their intention might not be good."

"Right, but at times, we just have to take a risk," Tycoma added.

POEM

One evening the two traveled along the shoreline and decided to take a rest at a rock. While resting Tycoma stood up tall, stared at the water, turned around and stared at Mamboya, then loudly proclaimed:

"I had a vision of a princess (queen)
who wept the pain out of my life with love.
Love was absent in every direction,
but your presence.
Your arms are like the safe refuge.
You're precious as the breath of life.
Your status says royalty.
You give me hope like the sunrise.
My life has no sunrise without you.
You're the life piece that mends my happiness.
You brighten darkness like the stars.
You're the reason I breathe the breath of life.
I've searched the four corners for you in my dream.
But now I see you in reality this day.
With patience we can see the stars.
So move closer to me and celebrate the festival of love.
You're worthy to me like water to a fountain.
You sustain my life.
Your path is my elevation,
because when I was trapped in the midst of loneliness and regret,
your presence restored love and faith within me.
So if a search for justice is unseen without sincerity,
I hope my modesty can search your soul and pierce your heart with love."

When he'd finished, she said, "Wow! How sweet!"

"Thank you," came Tycoma's reply.

"Is that for me?" she asked with a smile on her face.

"Well, you figure it out."

"Wow! Nice. No one has ever complimented me with such sentimental words to me before except my parents."

"Well, you're special. "

"Thanks, thanks a lot for caring," she said as she slowly kissed him on the lips.

"Wow!" he said with a huge smile on his face.

Chapter Four

"Our world is always different. We're not considered fit for survival. We are outcasts to the full grown humans. If captured by them, they'll enslave us or most likely kill us. So we are shadow walkers. We hide away from the light not to be seen, use our magical spells to be fast and swift with our feet and sneak out at night from our caves to steal food from the humans," Tycoma explained.

"Wow!" Mamboya said with her mouth wide open. "What a savage world."

"Oh yes, indeed," Tycoma replied, nodding his head.

"Oh nonsense, not all humans are like that," a voice said from the tree as a young boy climbed down.

"If you say so! Okay, here is my question for you. How come they always fight amongst themselves when they're the same people?"

"That's just survival nature. To overcome one must destroy the opposition," Saluku replied as he transformed into a snake.

Scared by the transformation, both Mamboya and Tycoma soon took off running, but they couldn't go further, because Mamboya quickly fell down causing Tycoma to halt. So Saluku surrounded her.

"Stop! I mean no harm. I come in peace. The world I'm placed in is full of criticism and judgment. I just want to be around people who won't judge me because of my status. I am a living creature, regardless of my shape."

"Okay, but you're a snake and a boy," Mamboya said.

"Yes, I am. But I have needs and emotions just like every creature that breathes. I mean no harm to you. I just want someone who understands me, and I thought you two would understand me being in the image that you are, but I guess not," Saluku explained calmly.

"No, no, no! Don't say that, we do understand you. It's just the flip side, you know snake and a human," Tycoma said.

"That is just my curse," Saluku replied as he transformed into a snake and wrapped around a mango tree.

"Curiosity is something that we all have. Whether we like it or not. It's a feeling that exists within us that leads to knowledge. The world of humans and strange creatures has always been paralyzed by plenty of mystery and few facts. Those that exist between the lines know the facts about both worlds.

"I love life, but I hate the world I came from," Saluku ranted with an angry look.

"Why?" Tycoma asked.

"Well, it's not like I hate them. But it is not a fair world."

"Quit stressing yourself. Life is not fair at times. A chicken can raise her chicks and a starving eagle can pick up her chick and turn it into a meal. So as you see life is not fair for us all," Tycoma explained.

"I know, Tycoma, but our world is so critical. We humans, whatever it is that we cannot see our reflection off, we try to eliminate. We hate competition. Sometimes we even misunderstand honor for an insult. For instance, someone can be a fan of us and we still hate them because we think they're trying to replace us.

"So we are always at war to exterminate competition, or those who oppose us. Even creatures who love us are often scared to be around us because of our savage ways. We exterminate anything in our way to feel superior.

"Humans are critical toward each other. They're always in pursuit to criticize and destroy others' principles and cunningly influence their ways into others' lives to enslave them. To me it is wrong because any educational practice that is enforced on people as a form of civilization is colonialism. And you who accept it have erased the tradition of your ancestry."

"You know what my grandfather always told me," Mamboya said.

"What?" Saluku also curious, asked with a question of his own.

"Curiosity can always lead to knowledge," she replied.

"Oh yes indeed. Your grandfather is absolutely right," Saluku replied.

"So tell me. What led you to the curse?" Mamboya curiously asked.

Saluku stared into the sky for a few seconds, and then at the ground before saying, "Well, it has been explained to me by my grandfather who also is a witch doctor. You see, my mother is a trader and she came from this village where cultural taboos are very strong. She broke a traditional taboo and took a bath in a stream that was forbidden for pregnant women. While taking a bath, a snake appeared beneath the water. Stunned by her vision she paused as the huge snake circled her three times, turned into a human, touched her belly, transformed back into a snake and swam back down to the bottom of the stream. My mother soon gave birth, and seconds after giving birth to me, I transformed into a snake. I crawled around her arms and lay back into her arms as a baby."

"How do you know all this?" Mamboya asked.

"Well, both my grandfather and my mother explained this to me."

"Whoa! I know she must have been frightened," Mamboya said.

"Yes, and I know because we supernatural creatures know our first memory of life," Saluku explained.

"Indeed. I remember mine too," Mamboya agreed.

The world they came from was different, so it made their bond strong because all three didn't view each other as a threat. They embraced each other as one and shared honest details with each other.

"Is it hard to live in regular human society?" Mamboya asked.

"Of course. It is not easy to live in a critical world. Their criticism and judgmental ways make it hard to take comfortable steps in their world. And like most normal humans, I wasn't the same as them.

"So I struggled to find my steps in the daytime. My speech was slow and so were my steps. My only words were, 'Mama' and "Eat'. And though I was viewed as an adorable child in the human world, I was an animal by night. During the night, I went through transformation and turned into a snake. During the full moon, I would become a snake and mingle with witches and strange mystical creatures."

"What makes you come in this direction?" Tycoma inquired.

"Well, because I want to be around those who don't criticize me. I like to be accepted the way I am and in their world, I can't obtain peace. Happiness and peace is what we all strive for in this life and wherever we can obtain it, is where our worth lies."

"Absolutely," Tycoma said as he bit the mango and climbed the coconut tree.

Chapter Five

Tycoma tricked Mamboya, casting a magic spell for her not to return back into the sea world. The sun soon rose and Tycoma couldn't cast away the spell for her to return back to the sea world.

Mamboya's parents were horribly worried. Her father searched the ocean and shoreline, but couldn't find any sign of her. Mamboya's cousin, Dafu, who was a source close to their daughter, soon pointed them in a helpful direction where she possibly could be.

Dafu told them that Mamboya wanted to see her friend by the shoreline and was still there.

Concerned for her safety, Mamboya's father, Taju decided to step into the human world to find his daughter who was trapped and couldn't return unless she was touched by someone from the sea world.

"Where could your cousin be?" Taju asked.

"I'm not quite sure, but she left me here this morning saying she was going to the shoreline to explore the world and see her friend."

"What friend?" Taju asked with a frown on his face.

"I don't know. I never saw her friend," Dafu said.

"This girl. I can't wait till I find her. The punishment I will give her."

"Come on, Taju. Find her first," Uncle Pewa said.

Adama Kohkoh was widely recognized throughout the town as the queen of witches. The rumor that was circulating around town was that she had sacrificed her first son to the devil for magical power and she would gain even more power if she killed her oldest sister in the next town.

As she aged, she went into a spiritual battle with a higher power. Hurt by this greater power, with her own power limited she sought a quest to regain her witch empire and would push any boundaries to gain superior ground. She ruled under the dark world for thousands of years, and a spiritual attack from a higher power was placed on her that forced her to lose her power. Her sister being successful overseas brought great distress to her because she wanted to be the daughter honored by her parents. So she recruited helpful puppet witches to regain her magic and reestablish her witch empire.

While Princess Mamboya was still trapped in the human world, the Queen of Witches Adama Kohkoh who was hurt by a spiritual attack heard of the princess' situation. She viewed it as a life restoration, so she immediately sent her witch guards to kidnap the princess to gain more magical power to destroy her sister Hawa.

Her agony, pain and discomfort is her joy, her failure is her success. As she struggled in the reality world to find comfort, she celebrated in the supernatural world. Adama Kohkoh burst into laughter. "Hahahaha. Now that the princess from the underworld is here, I can finally restore my power, crush my sister and rule again for a thousand years."

"Oh yes, you shall, Great One," Jokojeh said.

Tola the female witch guard, stood tall and licked her finger making a spark light up and said, "Indeed, Great One. You will be the Witch Queen and we will surely serve under your regime."

Adama Kohkoh smiled, stared at the sky and said, "I love the sound of that. But we can't allow time to set us back. We have to hurry up and set a trap and capture this princess."

"Hurrah! Hurrah! But what shall we do, Great One?" Tola asked.

"Oh yes, Great One. What shall we do now?" Jokojeh asked.

Adama stared into her kalabash and said, "You fly to the east and you to the west. I will travel center, north and south."

Chapter Six

"Oh hide, the flying saucers are out in the sky," Tycoma said with a terrified look on his face.

Shocked at his behavior, Mamboya stood confused, not knowing what to do.

"What shall we do?" she asked.

"Shhh. Just be quiet until they pass us," Tycoma said.

"Okay!" Mamboya answered in a squeaky tone.

The witches were flying high above in the sky with their brooms when Jokojeh paused and said, "Humm!"

"Oh, I thought I smelled a fish. I must be closer to the sea princess."

Tola then joined him and said, "We're surely close."

Jokojeh then smiled and flicked his fingers. "Oh yes, we will bring the princess to Queen Adama and she will honor us with thousands of beetles and flies."

"Oh how satisfying," Tola the female witch said crushing her teeth.

"Oh yes, I can't wait to crush on those yummy flies with some human blood," Jokojeh said.

"Hahahahaha. How satisfying," Tola celebrated with a joyful smile.

"Human blood and flies...aw yum yum!" Jokojeh rubbed his hands, flicked his nails and smiled.

(Song)
"We must go to find the princess.
We must act fast to gain power and get stronger.
We must move swiftly as a witch to capture and sacrifice the princess, so we can rule our empire once more."

The witch guards sang this song as they flew off in search of the princess, while the princess and her leprechaun friend rose from hiding.

"Queen Adama is ugly," Tycoma expressed as she threw a rock in the direction the witches were flying.

"She is not ugly. How can God's creation be ugly? Nothing created by God is ugly or should be criticized by men. Why? Because we cannot do better than our grand Creator."

"That makes sense, but some people are just too ugly."

"Depending on what you're looking for. Some have inner beauty."

"Beauty can only be defined by how one shapes it to be. There is physical beauty where status and image is all that matters, and there is also inner beauty where you're emotionally beautiful," Mamboya explained.

"Okay. I get your point. So who would you rather fall in love with, appearance or inner beauty?" Tycoma asked.

"Inner beauty of course!" she answered.

Chapter Seven

"Hide! Hide," Tycoma whispered.

"From who again?" Mamboya asked.

"The humans," Tycoma said with a fearful look on his face as two teen boys walked down a stream.

"Why?" she asked, growing more curious.

"Oh, you don't want to know. They're savages. They destroy anyone in their path."

"Why? Isn't anyone worthy for them to keep?" she asked.

"Oh yes, as slaves. If you're useful to their progress, they can surely keep you as their elevation steps up."

"Whoa! You guys lived in an insane world," she expressed in a carefree attitude as she walked away.

"Nah, they're just so mentally sick and obsessed for power and wealth that they can't take with them after death," he added.

"So why?" she asked again.

"That is an answer I can't give to you. All I know is, in our world, the less you have, the more humble you become, but in their world the less they have, the more obsessed they become."

"I guess they're vanity chasers," Mamboya said.

"They just like to feel superior. Even if it requires crossing others' boundaries to criticize and destroy an old foundation to establish their own principle, they will, which is to me more a concept of enslaving others. Their ways of civilization are to criticize and destroy an old foundation."

"Disaster world indeed."

"Hold that thought! Shh! They saw us, run! Come on, follow me," Tycoma said.

Without saying a word, Mamboya immediately took off running to join Tycoma in the same direction.

"Holly. Did you see that?" Bakar said.

"Yes, I did. Monsters. Let's go and go tell Papa," the younger boy said.

"I'm always curious how it is in your world. What is it like?" Saluku asked.

"Interesting question. My world is full of water and mysterious creatures deep beneath the blue ocean. It is a safe place for us marine wildlife to feast and survive, but it is also a hunting ground for humans since they're known to cross the boundaries of others for their own interest."

"Are you ashamed of yourself?" Mamboya asked.

"Ashamed? Nah. To live life you have to be prepared for the unexpected because reality can't always be tame or positioned in the manners of how we expect it to be. Reality is like the breeze, it is there and can be felt when it blows but you can't determine when it exists or where it will blow."

"That makes sense," Mamboya said.

"Oh yes, well, I live amongst humans so my mind has to work like them to survive," Saluku explained.

"So does this mean you have two brains?" asked Mamboya with a surprised look on her face.

"I don't know about two brains, but I live a double life between two worlds so I don't think like the average human or creature on the shoreline."

The shoreline was packed with creatures during the full moon, and the humans were starting to sight these creatures.

"Papa. Papa. I see something," Bakar said.

"Yes, Papa," the younger brother Abu agreed with his brother's claim.

"Oh you two have been drinking palm wind, huh?" the father asked.

"Papa, no. Papa, we did see a beautiful lady caver with leaves and a little leprechaun. Yes, Papa, we did," the boys answered.

"Where?" Sal asked.

"At Cape Sierra beach, but they took off running behind those rocks," the older brother explained.

"And yes, Papa they move fast," Abu said.

Sal smiled, shook his head and said, "Okay. Look, you two have a long day hunting. Go eat some meal and get some rest."

"We don't know exactly what they saw, but they both can't made up a creepy story like that," the mother said, coming to the boys' defense.

"Those boys are just hallucinating. Maybe from hunger, or maybe from drinking palm wine and chewing kola nut" Sal said.

"We raised them not to lie to us and I'm pretty convinced that they saw something or someone out there."

"Oh you're hallucinating too?" Sal asked as he burst into laughter.

"Not at all. I know how it feels to run to tell your parents something and they view us as insane. Trust me, my parents did the same thing."

"Look, woman, I don't have time for this. I have wood to finish chopping and go fishing," Sal said.

One beautiful evening, Sal decided to go fishing with his older son. As Sal and his older son, Bakar lay out their fishing line they saw the same creature there.

"Hey, Papa. Do you see that?" Bakar asked.

"Shh. I do. Be quiet so they won't hear us," Sal whispered.

"Exactly. That is exactly what we saw behind Cape Sierra."

"Oh shoot, they see us. They're running away. Where are they at?" the man asked.

"They're gone," Bakar answered.

"Wow!" Sal said with a spooked look.

"Yes, Papa. That's what me and Abu saw."

"Never doubt someone's vision," Sal quoted.

The father came home running after fishing with his son, crushing everything in his way to deliver the news.

"Hey guys, hey! I saw them," Sal said as he struggled to catch his breath.

"Saw what?" the mother asked holding his hands.

"Those creatures. I saw it with my own eyes when I came back from fishing with your brother," he explained as he continued struggling to catch his breath.

"Okay, hah!" he said as he pointed at Sal. "So now who is hallucinating?"

"I told you don't doubt someone's vision," she quoted with a smile.

"Now I know. And I'm sorry for not believing you, sons," Sal apologized.

"Hah! We told you so," Abu shouted with laughter.

"Yes, I should've know better not to doubt someone's vision," Sal said as he stared at the sky.

Chapter Eight

With Adama Kohkoh's growing concern over the princess she pulled out her mirror, swiped her hands over it and she saw both the princess and the leprechaun running.

"Nowhere to run," Adama Kohkoh whispered as she cast a magical spell to block their passage with a black cloud.

"Hold on! Don't panic. Just stay still," Tycoma said.

"What is that?" she asked.

"Don't move. I know how to rebuke it," Tycoma assured her.
"You do?" she nervously asked.

"Well, let's just hope this works," he replied as he sprinkled salt and a few magic words to clear the storm. The storm soon cleared and the two continued running. They ran until they couldn't run anymore.

"What do we do now and where do we go?" Mamboya asked.

"Nowhere," Adama Kohkoh replied.

"Run!" Tycoma yelled.

"Nowhere to run. So enough with the hide and seek games, kids," Adama Kohkoh said with laughter.

"Leave us alone you witch," Mamboya cried.

"Oh, him of course I will leave but not you. You're more worthy than any pearl or possession in this land."

Exactly as she stated she released the leprechaun and flew Mamboya back to her palace.

"Look you fish! Share your magical secrets with me or I will tear you into pieces."

"You're bluffing. You won't you crazy witch," Mamboya taunted her.

"Oh shut your mouth up. How dear you speak to our queen in such disrespectful words," the witch guard intervened to defend Adama Kohkoh.

"Oh you fool. You're just as useless as your master," Mamboya said provoking her with an insult.

"Watch your filthy mouth, young lady," Jokojeh said.

"No, just wait and let me shut it for her," Adama said.

Adama then said, "I thought she is useful, but I guess not. Let's just kill her and remove the load off our shoulders."

And as she lifted her hand to strike Mamboya with her knife the other guards intervened, held Adama's hands and said, "No. it won't benefit us. We waited all these years for an opportunity so we can regain what's ours and now that the opportunity is in front of us you want to destroy it?" Jokojeh said, incredulous.

"I completely understand, but I'm impatient," Adama said.

Chapter Nine

The sun didn't set on that particular day, and the pair arose from the sea world into Cape Sierra Beach in search of Princess Mamboya. Minutes into their search at Cape Sierra, they came across Saluku who was in a complete human form at that time and was sitting on a rock. The two mermaids immediately halted and sat alongside Saluku.

"Hey, young man, have you seen a young mermaid girl?"

"Oh, you mean Mamboya?" Saluku replied.

"Yes, do you know her whereabouts?"

"Not at this moment, but before I even say a word, who are you?" Saluku asked.

"Her relative. I am her father and that is her uncle," Taju answered.

"Okay. Well, I last saw her with my friend Tycoma."

"Tycoma. Who is that?" Taju asked.

"The leprechaun boy with magical power."

"Can you take us to him?" Taju asked.

"I would if I knew where he was, but unfortunately I don't. Sorry," Saluku replied.

"Sorry? No, please help us find my daughter," Taju desperately begged.

"Your daughter. Oh, she is indeed your daughter. You show sure great concern," Saluku said.

"Yes, she is my only daughter and I have to get her back home safe. Please," Dafu continued to beg.

"Please, you don't need to beg. We can find her by ourselves," Pewa bragged.

"Be quiet please, Ansu. We need help in a world that's not ours; we can't allow ego and ignorance to mislead us in a blind direction."

The three men continued their search quest.

"We have to cross this stream, but I can't swim," Tycoma said as he stared at the stream.

"You can't swim?" Uncle Pewa asked.

"You heard me. I can't. I'm not a fish!" Tycoma shouted with a frown.

"You don't have to be a fish to know how to swim."

"Look, we have to cross the river for me to take you where you want."

"How am I sure that you're telling us the truth and this is not a trap?" Uncle Pewa asked.

"Because she is my friend and they captured the both of us at the same time and since I'm not useful to their cause and ritual sacrifice, they let me go."

"What's so special about her?"

"Well, the witch needs to drink the blood of a sea creature with a distinct human and fish look."

"Why a mermaid?" the father asked.

"Not just any kind of mermaid. A female one. Tycoma."

With Adama Kohkoh not able to convince Mamboya to reveal her secret power to her, she went into transformation as Tycoma to conquer her spirit.

"Hey! Are you okay?"

"Yes, Tycoma. How?"

"Shh. It's alright. I'm here to rescue you."

"Wow. So you do care?" Mamboya said with a smile.

"Oh yes, my love," the disguised witch answered.

"My love? You never call me that," she said.

"Well that's your new definition."

"Okay. How weird."

"Yes, my love," Adama said.

"Okay, that's kind of corny now."

"How about Mamboya?"

"Okay, if you insist."

"Yes. Well, get me out of this chain and let's get out of here now," Mamboya pleaded as she yanked the chain on her hand.

"I can't."

With a surprised look on Mamboya's face, she shouted, "Why?"

"Because you have to reveal your deepest secret to me," the witch sneakily said.

"My deepest secret? That's weird, I already told you. Wait, wait, wait! You're not Tycoma."

"She is surely not," a loud voice from the corner sounded.

"What are you doing here in my palace?" Adama asked as she transformed back into her true identity.

"Oh, Tycoma. You really care!" Mamboya cried.

"I surely do and I will always," he responded with a tear running down his face.

"Hold that thought!"

They entered the palace. "We got one of them!" Jokojeh bragged.

Tycoma tried to run toward Mamboya, but Adama cast a spell on him that caused him to freeze.

"Mamboya!" Taju yelled.

"Papa! Let him go!" Mamboya screamed.

"Let my daughter go!" Taju yelled. He was trying to move, but he was tied up.

"Oh, how interesting to see a family affair."

"You crazy witch," Mamboya insulted Adama.

"How flattering," Adama said with a smile as she flicked her nail with her knife.

"Tie her down to the altar table. I need one string of her hair, one fingernail, and a drip of her blood before we kill her."

Uncle Pewa burst out of a corner and hit the witch with her broom and cast a spell on one of the two guards who quickly dropped to the floor. He rushed and untied his brother Taju.

As the witch guards fell down and hit the floor, Adama Kohkoh regained consciousness, rose up from the floor and cast a spell that unleashed a triple headed dog named Zoe. The creature immediately ran in Mamboya's direction to attack her, but Tycoma intervened and jumped onto the dog's back and got bitten on his leg. Taju didn't hold back. He got involved and grabbed the witch's sword and stabbed the dog and cut off all his heads.

"My leg, my leg!" Tycoma cried.

"Hold on, it's okay!"

"It's okay? "Tycoma asked with surprised look on his face.

"Yes, it's okay," she assured him as she crossed her hand over his wound and healed him.

"Wow! I'm healed. Thank you," Tycoma said.

"No, thank you for being here," Mamboya replied.

"You know what, Papa," Mamboya said.

"What is it my precious?" her father Taju asked.

"We can't know what awaits us until we take that life journey, and in life education and experience is civilization, so it is better to know something and don't act on it than to be ignorant about it and act on it in an unintended way. And we don't often see our value in life until tragedy strikes us. Tragedy is our life's revelation. It reveals to us those who will care for us at our perilous times and who are willing to cross boundaries. At times it can turn into emotion and sometime evolves into joy."

The two hugged. He then gazed into her eyes and said to her, "I am happy you're safe, my daughter."

"I am too, Papa," she replied with a smile.

While the two expressed their emotions, Tycoma turned around. "Well, I guess my job here is done. I messed it up and I fix it up. So I guess this is it," Tycoma said.

"But wait, Tycoma! This can't be it."

"Hey, reality is here now. I love you, but we are in different worlds."

"But wait, no, please!" Mamboya begged.

"Let's face it. As much as I want it to work, it won't," Tycoma said.

"It's not yet, son. I know our world is different, but Love has no limit when penetrating in the right direction. You proved to me you will go to any extent to rescue my daughter. So all I can say is take care of my daughter and keep her safe as you did today."

"Really?" he asked with a surprised look on Tycoma's face.

"Yes. Hey, after all, we are different creatures, but still breathing, right?"

"Oh yes. Papa, I love you even more." She jumped and celebrated.

"Yes. Yes! My dream is finally a reality," Tycoma celebrated with a smile.

Both the father and the uncle smiled and swam away from the shoreline while Mamboya kissed Tycoma and rejoined them. Tycoma watched them as the three disappeared beneath the sparkling blue waters of Cape Sierra Beach.

"Hate is a Disease that Love can Cure"

There once lived a rich man named Saidu, whose fortune and wealth was inherited from his rich farmer father who owned a coco plantation. As he grew in his early life, he studied the laws of business and maintained his inheritance. Though it was unfair to the poor, he still used the law of greed, through corporate rules, to enslave the less fortunate ones who begged him for the opportunity to gain enough resources to at least feed their loved ones.

He unfairly used the majority of his workers' time and benefited more off their labors to intentionally chain them to him.

Though his rich status and ego placed him above the average citizen, his rude manners and savage treatment made him the most hated man in town. The poor citizens of the town viewed and despised him as an evil and stingy man with no respect for lower class citizens. His view was "For one to be powerful, others have to pay a sacrifice of slavery." He never viewed life with equality.

But despite their opinion and complaints about his ways, he continued to do as he pleased. In his mindset, if his or any action benefited him, then that's all that mattered.

He lived and unfairly dominated this town despite the dislike of the citizens.

One morning Saidu decided to head to the suburbs with his driver Sakoy and assistant Jummah for a business meeting.

As he traveled on the highway to his meeting, his car broke down. They tried fixing it for hours, but they were unsuccessful.

The sun started to set, and it soon became too dark to work on the car. So, Saidu decided they should find the best hotel to lodge for the night. Saidu said that he was too rich to walk to that poor town, so he demanded that his two servants carry him on their backs until they found lodging.

The two men who were exhausted from the trip but still managed to carry Saidu on their backs around town until they found the best suitable hotel.

As soon as they found the hotel Saidu requested that he wanted their best room. And indeed he was granted the hotel's highest, most luxurious room.

He then requested his two servants to bring all his food to his room

They did as he said and stored all his food inside his room.

He offered them a little bit and kept the rest of the watermelon.

As they slept through the night a huge storm came and hit this little town and destroyed all of the plantations. The storm destroyed most of the foundation and the lower hotel rooms. The servants, staff, and guests all made it out alive. Saidu was also alive in the highest tower room with all of his watermelons.

The rich businessman laughed at the men and the rest of the hotel guests below him and daily he spit his watermelon seeds at them saying, "You poor lower class citizens deserve this."

Weeks into the mayhem, Saidu started to realize a problem ahead that would weaken him. "Nothing lasts forever," he cried. And he soon ran out of food. His laughter halted. His agony rose, and now it was him begging those beneath him for food to stay alive. Because the pumpkin seeds that he was throwing below them had grown into watermelons.

Though the majority opposed the idea of sharing their crops with him, some like his servants were still pitying him and decided to give him watermelons to sustain his life, saying, "We can't deal the hand of evil as our enemies and call ourselves saints. Hate is a disease that love can cure."

"Indeed," Saidu replied, with a satisfied look on his face as he nodded his head.

After a couple of days, help arrived. Saidu and his two servants immediately returned home. He asked his servant, Sakoy, "Why did you give me meals after I intentionally stole from your labor and starved you during the disaster?"

Sakoy smiled and said, "Not saying you're my foe, but sometimes in life you have to be bigger than your enemy to be their hero, like my grandfather always says."

"Your grandfather was a wise man."

"Oh yes. He surely was. But you know what, there are times we go beyond our ground to capture the things that matter to us or please those close by to our heart. Sacrifice is the testing ground to capture our destiny. It's the bridge we take through faith and at times risk unlocks our destiny."

Saidu stared at the sky for a few seconds before staring right into Sakoy's eyes saying, "You know the hardest pain is guilt. A mental disturbance that brings discomfort. I hate to tangle in a position where I can't help those that have been there for me nor knowing I can help someone, but refuse to and watch him or her suffer. I used to think if we all have equality then I'll have no choice but to be my own slave, but you know what? Fairness is good for all positive sides. If we all are perfect at what we're made for then the world won't go through agony and pain."

After their conversation Saidu became grateful to those around him. He understood that sharing is the key to growth. Treating each other fairly in society will bring happiness to all sides rather than to just one side. Because even the richest person needs help from someone below his or her status. So he decided to give sixty percent of his wealth away to those who had helped build it or contributed help toward him. Twenty-five percent to his two servants Sakoy and Jummah, ten percent to the hotel staff and guests from the hotel that fed him during starvation, and twenty-five percent to the rest of his workers, saying, "You can't see the lowest ground from the highest point."

Saidu acts of generosity led to more success for his business and those that he shared his wealth with. The community soon ignited with success because more avenue doors were opened through his sharing. Those who once despised him for his greed now viewed him as a good man of generosity. So trade resumed and profits rose as the sunrise. Happiness and success lit this city that once was torn by hate, anger and greed.

The Reason Why the Birds and Ants are Always After the Termites and The Worms

The reason why the birds and ants are always after the Termites and the Worms, is because long ago in the jungle when peace once existed amongst all the creatures, an act betrayal that seemed like an act of sportsmanship and kindness ignited a lifetime war between the sky and the ground. A sneaky plot executed by the starving termites and sneaky worms, but their sneakiness made them into the target by the golden eye of the earth and the strongest merchant. The protector of the ground and sky, the birds and the ants.

"I am hungry. My mouth is always itchy for something. I want to bite on something to feel my satisfaction," the termites said.

"I have the prefect idea. A festival with all the animals that can benefit both of us," the worm replied.

"Okay. How is that possible?" the termite asked.

"Look, I am a sneaky worm that loves crawling on a mess and you love to bite and turn things into a mess, right?" the worm asked.

"Yes. I don't like to see strength, that is why I destroy every foundation," the termite bragged.

"Exactly. We're the mess companion," the worm said.

The two bravely organized and executed their plan. And like dirt under a rug, their plan ended up destroying the foundation by the termites eating the foundation and causing the animals to crash and hurt themselves. With no escape from the trap, the birds and ants were sent to rescue all the animals rom the worm and termite's evil plans.

The ants and eagles' combination task force dominated the battlefield by exterminating and capturing those responsible for initiating the ambush, and then they withdrew with few left alive and dead captives as their reward. And so the eagle, Spyro, safely flew back to his nest.

The ants' army, on the other hand, encountered a problem on their own. An old blind pangolin, who heard about the ambush from a snail was sitting under a small river path and started to whistle to ease his hunger. curious to know, the ants set out to enquire the direction of the sound.
As they got closer, the blind pangolin became scared by the mysterious echo of footsteps.

So, he immediately stopped singing and pretended to be dead by laying on the ground and opening his shell. Instead of minding their business, the curious ants' army were still pumped up and feeling untouchable from their previous victory, so they took matters into their own hands and crawled all inside the pangolin shell. The pangolin then closed his shell, squeezing and crushing all the ants before eating all the ants, termites and worms.

And because of that, the ants and birds' arms declared war on the sneaky worms and itchy mouth termites.

LET IT FLY IF IT HAS WINGS
Freedom

There was a boy named Tik who went to the woods to explore. While he was exploring he saw a bird's nest high above in a tree. Seeing the nest amused this young explorer. So, he climbed the tree and looked inside and saw two eagle eggs.

He held both and tried to rush down before the eagle came back. But as he was climbing down one of the eggs dropped and broke!

Tik brought the egg home. A baby eagle egg soon hatched and Tik catered to the bird by feeding, bathing and keeping it inside her cage.

The chick was well taken care of all the way till maturity, and was happy.

Then, one day the bird got sick and Tik grew worried about the status of his beloved pet eagle. So, he continued to nurture the bird by feeding it and trying all kinds of medical treatments to cure it, but the bird was still laying down sick.

Tik got exhausted and fell asleep. As he wearily lay his head, he started to dream, and in this dream, he envisioned himself seeking help from a pet master. Tik explained his problem to the pet master.

The wise man answered him, "Our ability is useless without our freedom. Everyone needs freedom because freedom is happiness. You can't keep the bird in a cage forever. Let it fly if it can." The pet master words echoed in Tik's mind.

Suddenly, the pet master yelled, and Tik immediately woke up. He jumped from his bed and ran to get his birdcage. Dashing to the window, he opened it and let the bird fly away.

Burden From our Past

"There once lived a man named Kondoz, that does anything to gain material things to stay ahead and superior in life. Even if the task required him cheating or exterminating others' progress to gain his interests, Kondoz will.

"One night, as Kondoz lay his head to sleep, he died and suddenly journeyed to a cross path where he came to the pearly gates that lead to heaven."

"As he approached the pearly gates, he saw others whom had died and came to the afterlife, with flying wings flying across the pearl bridge to heaven.

"His eyes were amazed by what he saw, so he quickly jumped and immediately came right back down.

"Stunned from the disappointing result, he stood helplessly and soon realized that he didn't have flying wings to keep his feet above ground like the others above him; and worse was all his materials possession that he gained from his previous life hung heavy on him as a burden and making it impossible to cross the pearly bridge to heaven.

"Kondoz, realizing his efforts to elevate him to heaven like the others were helpless and he was clueless about the secret of having flying wings. So, he cried out to one of the angels, 'Why I don't have flying wings like the rest to fly across the pearly bridge?'

"The angel replied, 'All those with wings are those who value human lives rather than material things. In your previous life, material things are the main priority. It is what causes man to devalue others' lives and become self-god, but in our world, humanity is our first priority. Those are valueless. It will hang on you and make your human wings unseen and impossible to enter heaven.'

"Hearing those words, Kondoz stood in silence knowing his previous life had decided his fate.

"The Angel furthered the reasoning for the man's destiny by saying, 'Helping another individual create a solid path to progress, but cherishing material things over human lives proves to you the value of the material world more than the humanitarian world. All those with flying wings that are flying to the pearly gates of heaven are those that value humanity rather than vanity. Humanitarian acts is often uncredited in your previous satanic world, but they are always credited in God's heart. It is the wings that help you fly across to the pearly gate bridge to the heaven."

Words To My First Son

Today mark a day of celebration in my life
A day I graduate from a boy to a man.
A day I see reflection of my first seed
A day where my tears don't represent pain, but joy
A day when you became the brightest star in my life.
A day I proudly cut your umbilical cord
and change you first dipper as a father
May 13th 2010, you erase the pain from my mother death,
and replace it with joy as my prince.
That why I call you my reconstruction.
The nourishment to my happiness in life
because your birth liberate me from my parlous times as a boy
and gave a reason to stand in the light as a man.
So with you, I can proudly say, I am a father.
Since you fulfill the manly side of me.
That why I call you my greatest investment to society
because you're the layer to my future generation.

Extension of my Love

Extension of my Love
Just when I thought I've seen the glory of life,
I came to a reality point that blessing from the Almighty God is unlimited.
Because your presence has shown that love is an endless journey
you arched love and pierced my soul on July 12th 2012
The extension of love
You carry the bloodline to the future
You become the thread that strengthens brotherly love.
The golden prince that fills the void of royalty.

Acknowledgment

Thanks to the Almighty Lord God for making my dreams a reality.. Thank Him for the wisdom, strength. Thanks to my constructive parent Theophilus Bakanu and Raffiatu Kamara for the encourage and supportive toward progress. Thanks to my royal princes Theophilus Shaku and Tashiru Enoch Kamara for the inspiration to being a better man in life. Thanks to my loving sisters Augusta, Felleh, Nassimi, Sara, Felicia and my older brother James Kamara. Thanks to my entire family which include my cousins, nephew, niece, uncle aunty, grand parents, Oya Sesay, Kamafori Sillah, Sama Sesay, Alimamy Yande Kamara, Chief Pa Momo Sesay. Mammy Monday, Mammy Felleh, and all those that lend into my progress in life...Thanks to all the youth around the world that also spark inspiration for me to write these tales.."From my understanding as a writer, the best way to educate the youth is through meaningful tales or poetry, songs. Since we as parents can't or will never be perfect with our human ways all the time. So shearing constructive tales to elevate those around us or the generation ahead of us is progress steps in society".....I love you all for being the fuel in my life. Without your love, in other words inspiration, motivation through wise principles and courage, my engine wont run. You guys are the fuel to my progress. The signatures of my heart. I exceed through the reflection your moment. The root of inspirations. You nurture me like raining water pouring down a seed and watch me sprout growth like the sunrise.

I'll also like to give a special thanks to the mother of my sons, Haulatou Diallo, for her photograph contribution to this project. I also want to thank my friend and helper Darryl Sconies, Kima, Mike Vantino for the photograph, design and editing contribution.

76